Morris
in the Apple Tree

Collins

YELLOW

STORYBOOK

*Also by Vivian French
and Guy Parker-Rees*

MORRIS THE MOUSE HUNTER
MORRIS AND THE CATFLAP

Morris
in the Apple Tree

by Vivian French
illustrated by Guy Parker-Rees

CollinsChildren'sBooks
An imprint of HarperCollinsPublishers

First published in Great Britain by
CollinsChildren'sBooks in 1995

4 5 7 9 10 8 6

CollinsChildren'sBooks is
an imprint of HarperCollins*Publishers* Ltd,
77-85 Fulham Palace Road,
Hammersmith, London W6 8JB

Printed and bound in Great Britain by
Caledonian International Book Manufacturing Ltd,
Glasgow G64

0 00 674894 5

For Clyde, the real Morris
and for Pete – two really cool cats

Morris in the Apple Tree

Morris was ginger and white, and
very fat.

He was sitting in the sunshine and wondering if it was time for dinner.

"I'm sure it must be," he said to himself. "I'm very hungry."

He went inside to see if dinner was ready.

"GO AWAY," said his mother.
"You've only just had breakfast."

"Oh,"
said Morris.
He went
back to
sit in the
sunshine.

Morris cleaned his paws. Then he
cleaned his whiskers. Then he
cleaned his tummy.

"There," he said to himself. "It
must be time for dinner now."
He went inside to see.

"GO AWAY," said his big sister
Rose. "You've only just had
breakfast."

"But I've cleaned my paws," said
Morris. "AND my whiskers. AND
my tummy. And I'm hungry."

"GO AWAY!" said his mother and
Rose together.

Morris went.

Morris walked all
the way down to
the bottom of
the garden.
"It's not fair," he
said to himself.
"I keep myself
all clean and
tidy and they
won't give me
any dinner."
He went to sit
under the fence
with his back to
the house.
"It's just not
fair," he said. He
closed his eyes
and sulked.

"GRRRRRRRRRRRRRR!" There was a loud and terrible growl, and a large dog hurled itself at the fence from the other side.

"MEEEEEOW!" Morris leapt in the air.

"GRRRRRRRRRRRRRR!" The dog jumped up and down. Morris dashed for the nearest tree. He scrambled up it faster than he had ever scrambled anywhere.

Up and up he went, and out along
a branch. At the very end of the
branch he stopped.

"WOOF! Keep off my fence!" said
the dog, and it strolled away.

Rose and her mother heard the
dog barking.
"What's going on?" asked Rose.
"Perhaps you'd better go and see,"
said her mother.

Rose found Morris sitting in the apple tree. His fur was fluffed up all over. It made him look even fatter than usual.

"Whatever are you doing up there?" asked Rose.
"Sitting," said Morris.

"I can see THAT," said Rose, "but WHY? You don't like sitting in trees."
"I know," said Morris. "I was chased."

"CHASED?" Rose stared at him.
Morris nodded.
"Morris," Rose said, "come down
here and tell me what happened."

"I can't," said Morris. "I'm stuck."
"Oh," said Rose. "Are you sure?"
Morris stood up on his branch, and
it wobbled.

"MEEEEEOW!" he shrieked, and
he held on tightly with all his paws
and claws.

"Just jump!" Rose said.

"I can't!" Morris sat down again.
"I'm stuck."

Rose looked at the tree. It looked a very easy tree to climb.

"Why don't you just turn round and climb back down?" she asked. Morris shivered.

"I CAN'T turn round," he said.
Rose sighed. "Oh Morris," she said,
"it's easy! I'll show you!"

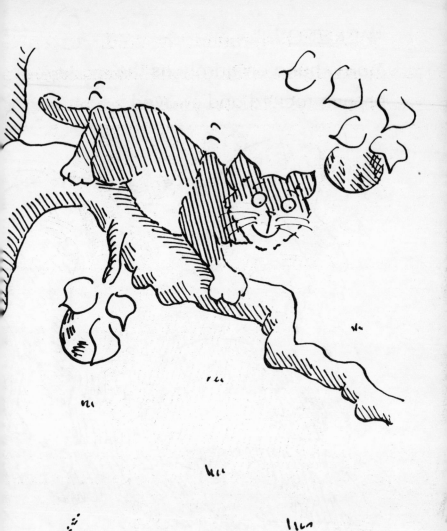

She sprang up the tree and
stalked along Morris's branch.

"MEEEEOW!"

Morris hung on grimly as the branch rocked and swayed.

"Now," said Rose as she sat down beside Morris. "All you have to do is turn round and you'll be back on the ground in no time!"

Morris shook his head.

Rose stood up. "Look, I'll turn right round so you can see how easy it is."

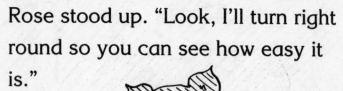

Morris nodded.

There was a pause.

"Well," said Rose, "it SHOULD be easy enough."

There was another pause.

"Morris," said Rose. "I can't turn round."

"No," said Morris.

"Am I stuck?" Rose asked.

"Yes," said Morris.

Their little brother Tom came
bouncing out of the bushes.

"Hello Morris," he said. "Hello Rose.
Why are you sitting in that tree?"

"We're stuck," said Morris.
"We can't get down."

"I could get down," said Tom. "If I
was stuck in that tree I could just
jump down. I'm good at jumping."

"It's a very long way," Morris said.

"No it isn't," said Tom. "Not if you're good at jumping. I'm VERY good at jumping. Look!"

He scrambled up the tree and appeared beside Rose. The branch shook and trembled.

"MEEEEEOW!" said Morris as he swayed to and fro. "HELP!"
"TOM!" said Rose. "Get down AT ONCE!"

Tom stood up on the branch.
"I'm going to jump," he said.
"Watch me jump, Morris.
Watch me jump, Rose."

"You be careful," said Rose.
"Scramble down the way you
came up."
Morris shut his eyes.

"WATCH ME JUMP!" said Tom.

Morris opened one eye.

Rose held her breath.

Tom suddenly sat down.

"Actually," he said, "I think I'll
jump in a little while."
"Tom," said Rose, "turn round
and go down NOW!"

Morris opened the other eye.
"He can't," he said. "He's stuck
too."

"I'm not," said Tom. He wriggled a little. "Well, I'm only a little bit stuck."

"Merrrow!" said Morris. "KEEP STILL!"

The three kittens sat close together on the branch. It was very quiet in the garden.

Morris sighed heavily. "We'll be here for ever and ever," he said.

"Will we really?" asked Tom.

"No," Rose said. "Mother will come
and find us very soon."

The three kittens went on sitting.

"Is it very soon yet?" asked Tom.

"I don't think so," said Rose, "but I'm sure it won't be long."

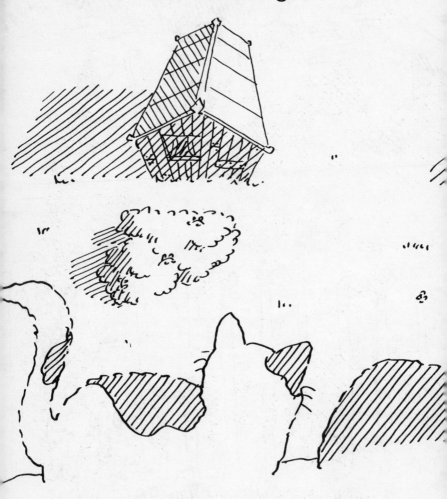

"I'm hungry," said Morris.

"You're always hungry," said Rose.
"Shall we call for Mother?" asked
Tom.

"I think she's too far away to
hear," said Rose.

"She's probably getting our dinner ready," said Morris.

Tom began to cry. "Meeeeow. Meeeeow. MOTHER!"

"WOOF! WOOOF! WOOOOF!"
There was a loud barking from
the other side of the fence
below the tree.

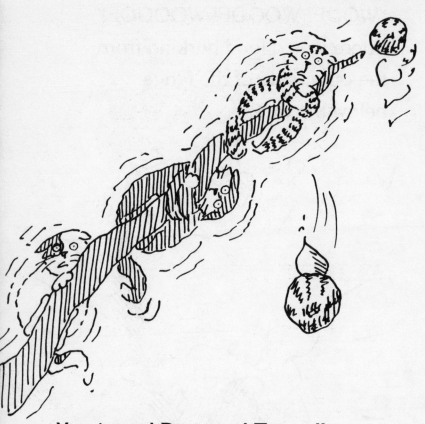

Morris and Rose and Tom all
trembled and the branch swayed
wildly to and fro. The three kittens
held on desperately, their paws
clutching and their ears flattened.

"HELP!" Rose shouted.

"MOTHER!" yelled Tom.

"MEEEOW!" howled Morris.

The dog stopped barking and
snuffled through the wooden slats.

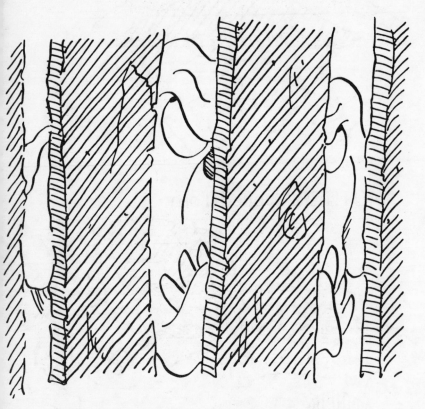

"Woof. What are you doing up
there? This is MY fence."
He caught sight of Morris.
"WOOOF! I told YOU to buzz off!"

He began barking again.

"YAH! BOO! I'LL CATCH YOU!
SCAREDY CATS, SITTING IN A
TREE, COME DOWN HERE AND –"

"PSSSSSSSSSSST!" Mother Cat arrived in a flying bundle of claws and teeth and fluffed up fur. She leapt at the fence, and the dog let out a loud howl and disappeared. "MOTHER!" Morris and Rose and Tom stared down at her with wide open eyes.

"You are brave!" said Rose.

"I want
to go home!"
said Tom.
"Is dinner ready?"
asked Morris.

Mother Cat sat down and looked up at the tree. Her eyes were narrowed and her tail was twitching.

She did not look at all pleased to see them.

"If there's a way up," she said,
"then there's ALWAYS a way
down. Tom, turn round and come
down here AT ONCE!"

"Yes, Mother," said Tom meekly,
and he turned round and
scrambled down the tree.

As he arrived on the ground
Mother Cat cuffed him with her
paw and sent him flying back up
the path.

"Now you, Rose," said Mother Cat.
Rose stood up. Morris wrapped his
paws round the branch and dug
his claws in. Rose wobbled round,
and then ran along the branch and
down to the ground.

"Fancy a great big kitten like you getting stuck!" said Mother Cat. Rose scampered up the path after Tom.

"Now you, Morris," said Mother Cat.

Morris clung on and shut his eyes.
"I can't," he said.

Mother Cat looked at him. "How
did you get up there?" she asked.

"I was chased," said Morris.
"And now I'm stuck."

Mother Cat nodded. "Hmmm," she said. "Well, if you're stuck, you're stuck. But it's a pity." She stood up and stretched.

"Your dinner is all ready. It's fresh sardines and your favourite kitty crunchies."

Morris opened his eyes wide.
Mother Cat was rubbing her back
against the fence.

"And there's a bowl of cream. Of
course, by now Tom and Rose
may have eaten it all..."

Morris jumped. He arrived on the
ground in a large fluffy heap.

"Goodness me," said Mother Cat.
Morris didn't hear her. He was
hurrying up the path, his tail held
high.